For my parents, Duncan and Sylvia, and my sister, Yvonne

First published in the United States 1996
by Dial Books for Young Readers
A Division of Penguin Books USA Inc.
375 Hudson Street
New York, New York 10014

Published in the United Kingdom 1996
by David Bennett Books Limited

Library of Congress Cataloging in Publication Data available upon request.
ISBN 0-8037-2075-0

The art for this book was rendered in oil.

Christmas
with
Teddy Bear

Jacqueline McQuade

Dial Books for Young Readers New York

Counting down to Christmas

Teddy Bear could hardly wait for Christmas.
He sat with his cat and crossed off
another day on his calendar.

Looking in Christmas windows

Teddy liked to go into town with his dad.
He loved the brightly colored toys in the toy store window,
especially the yellow airplane.

Building
a snowman

Teddy built a big snowman with coal for eyes
and a carrot nose. He gave him a hat and
a wool scarf to keep him warm.

Writing to Santa

"Dear Santa," wrote Teddy. "I have been a good bear this year. For Christmas I would like a toy airplane. I will leave a snack by the fireplace—milk and cookies for you, and a carrot for Rudolph."

Singing carols

One snowy evening Mom and Dad took
Teddy caroling. They sang his favorite Christmas songs
and then went home for hot chocolate.

Decorating the tree

Teddy and his dad decorated the tree together.
Teddy proudly put the last ornament on the very top:
the star he'd made the year before.

Making Christmas cards

Teddy made two cards, one with a tree for Mom and one with a snowman for Dad. After carefully coloring them in, he and his cat signed them with a kiss and a paw print.

Wrapping
a present

Teddy got some colorful wrapping paper and
a long, silky ribbon. With his cat's help
he remembered how to tie a big, beautiful bow.

Hanging
the stocking

Before bedtime on Christmas Eve, Teddy hung his
stocking above the fireplace where he knew Santa would
find it. He imagined all the things it would be
filled with in the morning.

Looking for Santa's sleigh

Teddy was so excited, he couldn't sleep.
He looked out at the starry sky,
hoping to see Santa's sleigh.

Opening presents from Santa

Early Christmas morning Teddy ran to the living room
and found his stocking overflowing with presents.
Poking out of the top was the yellow airplane.

Giving
a present

"Merry Christmas,"
said Teddy as he gave his cat a special gift.
"I love you."